ROBYN HOOD

ROBYN HOOD
THE CURSE

Writer **CHUCK DIXON** Artwork **JULIUS ABRERA**

Colors **ROBBY BEVARD** Letters **TAYLOR ESPOSITO (OF GHOST GLYPH STUDIOS)**

Editor **DAVE FRANCHINI** Art Direction & Design **CHRISTOPHER COTE**

Cover Artwork **IGOR VITORINO & KYLE RITTER**

Grimm Universe created by **JOE BRUSHA & RALPH TEDESCO**

This volume reprints Robyn Hood: The Curse issues 1-6 published by Zenescope Entertainment.
First Edition, November 2018 • ISBN: 978-1942275817

WWW.ZENESCOPE.COM

Joe Brusha • President & Chief Creative Officer
Ralph Tedesco • VP Film & Television
Christopher Cote • Art Director
Dave Franchini • Editor
Christina Barbieri • Assistant Editor
Ashley Vanacore • Graphic Designer
Lauren Klasik • Director of Sales & Marketing
Jennifer Bermel • Business Development & Licensing Manager
Jason Condeelis • Direct Sales Manager
Laura Levandowski • International Project Coordinator
Rebecca Pons • Marketing & VIP Coordinator
Stu Kropnick • Operations Manager

THE STORY SO FAR

After being orphaned as a teen and suffering a brutal attack that left her missing an eye, Robyn Locksley was transported to the realm of Myst where she liberated the city of Nottingham from its corrupt rulers. Now back home in New York City, with her unmatched skills and proficiency with a bow, she patrols the streets as both private investigator and vigilante, taking on cases and evils too dangerous for the average person...while stopping to save the world on numerous occasions—in her spare time, of course.

zenescope
ROBYN HOOD
THE CURSE
1
DIXON
ABRERA
BEVARD
ESPOSITO
COLAPIETRO
'17
LAUNCH

THE COPS IN NEW YORK ARE GOOD.
BUT SOMETIMES THEY DON'T KNOW WHAT THEY'RE LOOKING AT.
LIKE WHAT THEY SEE AS A RASH OF GANG SLAYINGS--
--I SEE AS A PATTERN OF RITUAL MURDERS.

THESE MOOKS AREN'T YOUR TYPICAL GANGBANGERS.
I CAN SMELL IT ON THEM.
SULFUR AND BLOOD.
THEY'RE FROM SOUTH OF THE VILLAGE.
WAY SOUTH.
DAMN.
SOMEWHERE IN THE NEIGHBORHOOD OF HELL.

SURE, NARCO GANGS ARE INTO SOME UGLY STUFF.
THEY DON'T USUALLY DRAIN THEIR VICTIMS OF BLOOD...
...THEN USE THE BLOOD TO PAINT BASTARDIZED LATIN PHRASES DOWN THE MIDDLE OF BLEECKER.
THESE GUYS ARE ALL WRONG.
YOU RIGHTEOUS LITTLE COW!
GOOD THING I DIPPED THESE ARROWHEADS IN A FONT AT ST. PATRICK'S.
YOU BITCH!

WHAT ROCK--WHAT CIRCLE OF HELL DID YOU CRAWL FROM?
HIH... HIH....
DOESN'T MATTER NOW, SWEETIE. THE LINE BETWEEN THIS WORLD AND THE NEXT IS ABOUT TO BLUR.
RIDDLES? SERIOUSLY? HOW ABOUT ANOTHER SHAFT WHERE IT'LL REALLY HURT?
HIH... HIH...HIH...
SOMEONE'S COMING...HIH... HIH...HIH...
SAN DIEGO.
YOU SURE YOU'VE NEVER DONE THIS BEFORE?
I'M SURE! I TOLD YOU, I'M A VIRGIN AT THIS, OKAY?

WE'VE TALKED ABOUT THIS FOR AGES. IT'S TIME WE TRY IT.
AS LONG AS YOU KNOW IT'S VERY, VERY NAUGHTY, SAM.
NAUGHTY, HELL!
IT'S DAMNED DANGEROUS, MARIAN.
AS LONG AS WE BOTH WANT IT. THAT'S THE ONLY WAY THIS WORKS.
CONSENTING ADULTS. I GET IT.
TOO LATE TO TURN BACK NOW. WE'RE ALMOST--

--DONE.

I'LL START. EXCUSE THE TRANSLATION. MY ARABIC IS RUSTY.
PH'NGLUI MGLW'NAFH C'RUTHU R'LYEH WGAH'NAGL FHTAGN.
PH'NGLUI MGLW'NAFH C'RUTHU R'LYEH WGAH'NAGL FHTAGN.
O'LU'GHTH KAH'LAR'JAMA, JAME KAH'LARRA DIN. DIN O'LU N'GTHAR C'RUTHU.
O'LU'GHTH KAH'LAR'JAMA, JAME KAH'LARRA DIN. DIN O'LU N'GTHAR C'RUTHU.
GODDESS!
IT'S BEAUTIFUL.

NO, NOT BEAUTIFUL, SAM. HIDEOUS. MALIGNANT.
THE STARS. THEY'RE ALL UNKNOWN TO US. CONSTELLATIONS I'VE NEVER SEEN BEFORE.
IT'S SOMEWHERE FAR FROM HERE. AT THE EDGE OF THIS UNIVERSE OR THE NEXT.
OR EONS IN THE PAST OR FUTURE, OR A PLACE BEYOND TIME. BEYOND THE RULES OF OUR REALITY.
"WE NEED TO END THIS, SAM. WE NEED TO CLOSE THE PORTAL NOW."
"JUST ANOTHER MINUTE, MARIAN. WE WORKED SO HARD TO GET HERE."
"LET'S ENJOY THE SHOW A LITTLE MORE."

SAM!

NO...

KEEP *BREATHING*, SAM! STAY WITH ME!

I'LL GET *HELP*, BABY... THOUGH I'M NOT SURE WHAT TO *TELL* THEM...

NINE-ONE-ONE. WHAT IS YOUR EMERGENCY?

AMBULANCE! I NEED AN *AMBULANCE!* SEVEN-THREE-SEVEN BALBOA. APARTMENT THREE-OH SEVEN! *HURRY!*

SAN DIEGO NATURAL HISTORY MUSEUM.
FORGET SOMETHING, DR. HUTCHISON?
HRM UHM.
HOLLER IF YOU NEED HELP, OKAY?
ARCHIVAL ROOM B-4
98% FACIAL RECOGNITION MATCH. HUTCHISON, JAMES LEWIS, DR

HERMOSA...
HEY, DOC. YOU KNOW YOU NEED TO SIGN IN TO--
DOC?

MORNING.
YOU CAN HAVE HIM IN TWENTY MINUTES, MOSE.
MAKE IT TEN, HAL.

OUR ACTOR HAS AN EIGHT-TO-TEN-HOUR JUMP ON US.
IT'S A STABBING RIGHT? LOOKS LIKE A STABBING.
MORE LIKE A GUTTING, JACK.

LAST PERSON REGISTERED TO COME INTO THIS ROOM IS A DR. HUTCHISON. TWO-TWENTY-NINE THIS MORNING.
I'LL HAVE A UNIT MEET US THERE.

THIS IS A WEIRD ONE, JACK.
I HATE THE WEIRD ONES.

CHANGED MY MIND, JACK.
THIS IS A @#$%ING WEIRD ONE.

IS THIS WHO I *THINK* IT IS?
DR. JAMES LEWIS HUTCHISON, I'M GUESSING.
HROOP!

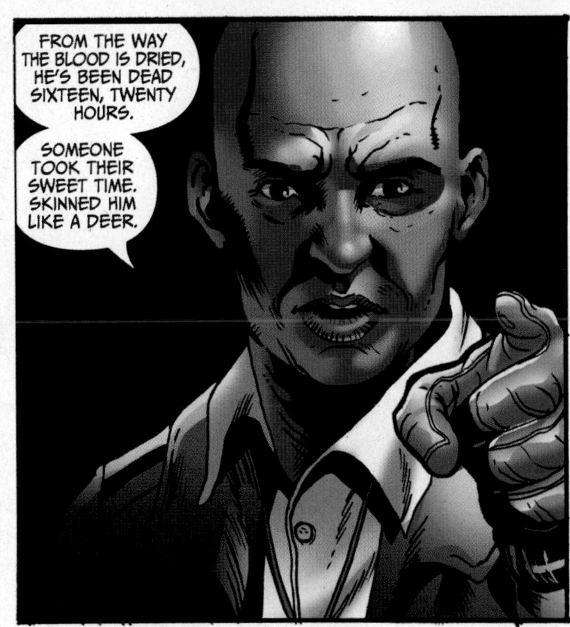
FROM THE WAY THE BLOOD IS DRIED, HE'S BEEN DEAD SIXTEEN, TWENTY HOURS.
SOMEONE TOOK THEIR SWEET TIME. SKINNED HIM LIKE A DEER.

THINK HE WAS *ALIVE* AT THE TIME?
THERE'D BE MORE *BLOOD* IF HE WAS ALIVE WHEN THEY DID THIS, RIGHT?

BUT THE FACIAL *RECOGNITION* PROGRAM RECOGNIZED HIM MILES AWAY AND HOURS LATER.
YEAH. HOW'S *THAT* WORK?

I THINK OUR ACTOR SKINNED THE DOC THEN *WORE* HIM TO THE MUSEUM.
HRAWWP!

MAN, I *HATE* THE WEIRD ONES.

YELLOW CAB
WHAT'S IN THE CASE? A HARP?
A BOW.
YEAH?

COMPETITION OR HUNTING?
HUNTING.
TAXI
WHAT ARE YOU HUNTING IN SOUTHERN CALIFORNIA?

NOT SURE YET.

MARIAN.

OH, ROBYN.

WHAT HAPPENED TO SAM?
I'M NOT SURE.
MARIAN.

OKAY.
WE GOT A LITTLE MORE INVOLVED THAN WE SHOULD HAVE IN AN AREA OF MAGIC A LITTLE DARKER THAN WE'RE USED TO.

HOW DARK?

BLACK AS SIN, ROB.
AN OLD BOOK IN ARABIC AND... SOME OTHER LANGUAGE. SOMETHING TOUCHED SAM. SOMETHING OLD.

I'VE DOOMED HER. AND DAMNED HER.
IT WAS SAM'S DECISION TOO.
I SHOULD HAVE STOPPED IT.

"I COULD HAVE STOPPED IT."

HEY, DARLING. IT'S ME AGAIN.

YOU LOOK LOVELIER THAN LAST NIGHT, SAMANTHA.

REMEMBER LAST NIGHT?
I PROMISED YOU SOMETHING.

SHAME YOUR MOUTH'S COVERED LIKE THAT.

WHOA!

HEY, YOU'RE AWAKE, HUH?
MAYBE YOU'D LIKE TO--
HUH?
NO!

WHAT DO YOU MEAN YOU DON'T KNOW WHERE SHE IS? SHE WAS IN A COMA!
NO ONE SAW HER LEAVE, MISS.
DON'T BLAME THEM. THEY DON'T HAVE ANY ANSWERS, MARIAN.

YOU HAVE A BOND WITH SAM. USE THAT. USE YOUR TALENTS.
YES. I CAN FIND HER.

IF THERE'S A FLICKER OF HER ESSENCE, I'LL SEE IT.
SPECULUM SIDERUM MEA OSTENDE MIHI...

LOOK, SHE'S STRESSED. YOU UNDERSTAND. IS THERE ANYTHING ON THE SURVEILLANCE CAMERAS?
YOU COULD CHECK WITH SECURITY. WE'VE CALLED THE POLICE.

THERE'S NOTHING!
YOU MEAN SHE'S DEAD?
NO! NOTHING! LIKE SHE NEVER EXISTED!

EXIT
YOU'RE *TIRED*, MARIAN. I'LL TAKE YOU *HOME*.
YES. MY BOOKS AND TALISMANS ARE THERE. I CAN BROADEN MY PSYCHIC SEARCH AREA.

ONLY IN CALIFORNIA.
RIGHT?

I'LL GET US AN UBER.
WHAT, YOUR *BROOM'S* IN THE SHOP?
FUNNY. YOU'D HAVE HAD THEM IN *STITCHES* AT SALEM.

WE'LL *FIND* HER. TOGETHER.
WILL WE, ROBYN?
I'M A *HUNTER*, REMEMBER? FINDING THINGS, PEOPLE EVEN, IS MY *THING*.

THIS *WON'T* BE AS SIMPLE AS FINDING A TRAIL OR FOLLOWING A SCENT.
WE *MESSED* WHERE WE SHOULDN'T HAVE BEEN MESSING. THIS IS *BAD*.

SO, IT GOT *CRAZY*.
WE'VE DONE CRAZY BEFORE.

YOU ARE A LIAR! YOU MADE A PROMISE!
MY HUMBLE APOLOGIES, CARLOTTA. I KNOW I AM LATE.
EVEN THE GREAT GERMÁN VILLARAIGOSA MUST KEEP HIS PROMISES!
A DAY LATE, CABRÓN!
I WILL AKE IT UP O YOU.
A MASERATI?
WHAT COLOR?
RED.
OF COURSE.
NOW EXCUSE ME UN MOMENTO, CARLOTTA.

MAN, I'M TIRED. AND MY FEET HURT. AND THIS BAG IS HEAVY.
AND WHOSE FAULT IS THAT?
LIKE IT'S MINE?
YOU SPENT OUR TROLLEY FARE, DUDE! YOU'RE WHY WE'RE WALKING!
SHEAH! LIKE I WASN'T GOING TO BUY THAT PRIMO HAWKWOLF NUMBER ONE!
YOU CAN'T BE--
UHHHH...
IS SOMEONE THERE?
ARE YOU OKAY?
HOO.
I THINK SHE'S DRUNK.

ARE YOU SICK?
AND WHO ARE YOU DRESSED AS?
GAAAAAAH!
AWESOME COSPLAY!
TO BE CONTINUED

ROBYN HOOD

zenescope
2
ROBYN HOOD
DIXON
ABRERA
BEVARD
ESPOSITO
THE CURSE

SAN DIEGO IS A BIG CHANGE FROM MANHATTAN.
PALM TREES. AWESOME WEATHER. A SLOWER PACE.
IT'S A DIFFERENT CITY, SAME OLD PROBLEMS.
WHERE WOULD SAM GO, MARIAN? DID SHE HAVE ANY FAVORITE PLACES?
I TRIED ALL OF THEM, ROBYN.
ZIP. ZERO. NADA.

WELL, AS MUCH AS I LIKE TOURING THE CITY BY CYCLE...
I'M DOING THE BEST I CAN. THIS LOCATION SPELL SHOULD WORK.
A MYSTICAL STAR 69?
SORT OF. IT HELPS ZERO IN ON ANY SOURCES OF SUPERNATURAL ENERGY.
AFTER OUR FAILED EXPERIMENT, SAM SHOULD BE PULSING WITH THE STUFF.
THAT IS AMAZING, MAR.
IT'S REALLY ONLY A SIMPLE SPELL.
I MEAN THE 4K RESOLUTION ON THIS PHONE. WHO'S YOUR CARRIER?
18TH A.
HYSTERICAL.
TURN LEFT AT THE NEXT CORNER.
YOU GETTING A PING ON YOUR WITCH-DETECTOR?
IT'S ONLY A GLIMMER.

"BUT IT COULD BE SAM."
YOUR CAR, SIR?
BLACK PORSCHE.
SURE. SURE.
UM...
THE PARKING LOT IS *THIS* WAY, AMIGO.
WHAT IS IT, GERMÁN?
SOMETHING'S NOT *RIGHT* HERE.
SPAK
SPAK
SPAK
SPAK
SPAK
SPAK
SPAK
SPAK
DOWN!
SPAK

¿ES ÉL?
¡ES LA BRUJO! ¡MÁTALO!
WHO ARE THEY?
I HAVE NO IDEA, MI VIDA!
LA VENGANZA DE DIOS ESTÁ SOBRE TI, MONSTRUO!
MALDICIÓN!
AGHK!
SHUK
SHUK

I DISARMED THEM. IT COULD HAVE ENDED RIGHT THERE.
THEY CHOSE TO GO MAKE THE GAME LETHAL.
SHUK
SHUK
PUTA!
EH?
THUNK

LEAVING THIS ONE ALIVE TO TALK TO ME.

OR TO THE COPS.

DAMN.

YOU! SHOW YOUR HANDS!

I PAID YOUR BAIL, MS. LOCKSLEY.
YOU'RE THE GUY THOSE SICARIOS WANTED DEAD.
SICARIOS? NO. NO. NO.
THEY WERE SIMPLY HOLD-UP MEN.
WITH THAT KIND OF FIREPOWER? DID YOU MANAGE TO GET THE COPS TO BELIEVE THAT, SENOR VILLARAIGOSA?
YOU KNOW ME?
ONLY FROM POP MAGAZINE.
RICHEST MAN IN MEXICO. SIXTH RICHEST IN THE WORLD. OIL. REAL ESTATE. ENTERTAINMENT.
DO YOU NEED A RIDE? YOUR MOTORCYCLE IS AT THE IMPOUND YARD. IT'S A BAD NEIGHBORHOOD.
BUT THEN, WHO AM I TALKING TO?
ONLY IF I DRIVE. I DON'T RIDE WITH STRANGE MEN.
BUT YOU KNOW ME FROM THE MAGAZINES.
AND FROM WHAT THEY WRITE, I MIGHT JUST LEAVE YOU STANDING HERE.

ROBYN? WHO'S THIS GUY?
ROBYN?

SAM'S MISSING AND SHE'S JOYRIDING WITH SOME MALE COUGAR.

OH, SAM...
WHERE ARE YOU?

CORONADO ISLAND.
NAVAL AMPHIBIOUS BASE.
YOU SEE WHAT I SEE?

IT'S A CHICK!
WHAT'S SHE DOIN' SWIMMING OUT THERE?
SHE AIN'T SWIMMING, DUMBASS.

SHE'S *DROWNING!*
MAN'LL DO *ANYTHING* TO MEET A HOTTIE.
YOU SHOULD TRY ONLINE DATING, BRO. IT'S DRIER.

HOLD *ON*, MISS!
I'M *COMING!*

DENNIS!
WHAT *IS* THAT?
WHAT THE HELL? *WHAT THE HELL?*

THANKS FOR THE USE OF YOUR RIDE.
WAIT, MS. LOCKSLEY, I HAVE NOT PROPERLY THANKED YOU FOR SAVING MY LIFE.

THIS BETTER BE GOOD, MONROE.
YOU CAUGHT THE CASE WITH THE VIC WHO GOT SKINNED, RIGHT?
AND WHAT'S THIS GUY HAVE TO DO WITH THAT?

HE CAN'T SHUT UP ABOUT IT. BABBLING ON ABOUT RITUAL SACRIFICE AND ANCIENT MEXICAN MAGIC AND CRAP LIKE THAT.
GREAT. YOU BROUGHT US ACROSS TOWN TO TALK TO A MENTAL PATIENT.
10341
THIS GUY ATTACKED THAT BILLIONAIRE GUY, HUH?

YEAH. BUT YOUR VIC GETTING FLAYED NEVER MADE THE NEWS.
YEAH.
HE KNOWS ALL ABOUT IT. AND THE WEAPON USED ON THE MUSEUM GUARD.

10341
HE HAS TO BE STOPPED. YOU HAVE NO IDEA OF HIS POWER!
WHO WE TALKING ABOUT, JORGE?

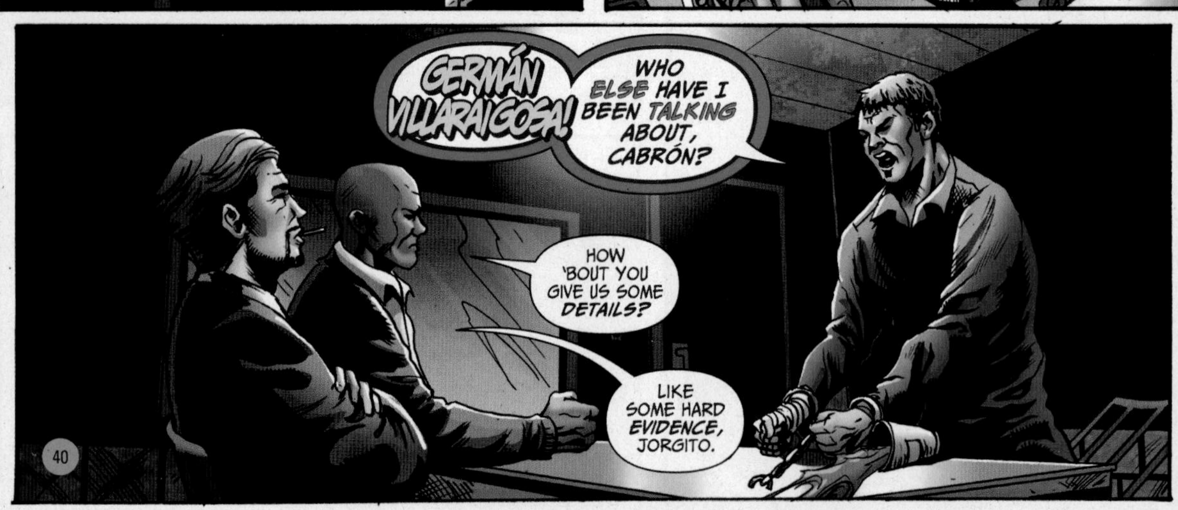
GERMÁN VILLARAIGOSA!
WHO ELSE HAVE I BEEN TALKING ABOUT, CABRÓN?
HOW 'BOUT YOU GIVE US SOME DETAILS?
LIKE SOME HARD EVIDENCE, JORGITO.

THE MAN AT THE MUSEUM. HE WAS KILLED WITH A SACRIFICIAL DAGGER WITH A QUARTZ BLADE.
THE MUSEUM DIRECTOR WAS SKINNED SO THAT HIS KILLER COULD WEAR HIM AS A DISGUISE.

THAT CONFIRMS WHAT THE M.E. FOUND. FLAKES OF QUARTZ IN THE GUARD'S WOUNDS.
WHY WEAR THE *WHOLE* SKIN? WHY NOT JUST THE *FACE?*

I *TOLD* YOU. IT IS *ALL* A PART OF THE RITUAL.
VILLARAIGOSA IS A HIGH PRIEST. HE SEEKS POWER. THAT MEANS FOLLOWING EVERY STEP OF THE RITUAL.

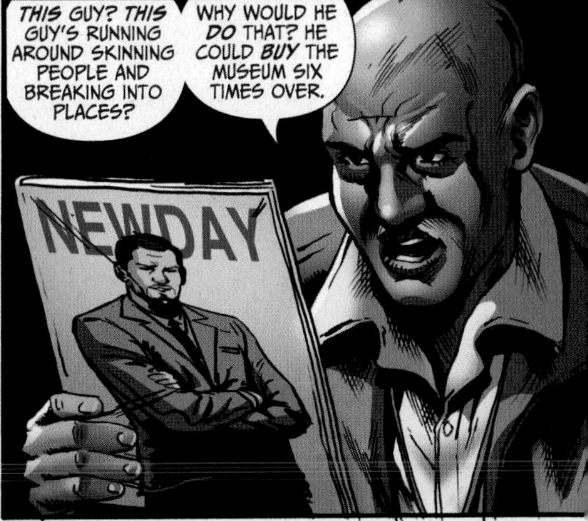
THIS GUY? *THIS* GUY'S RUNNING AROUND SKINNING PEOPLE AND BREAKING INTO PLACES?
WHY WOULD HE *DO* THAT? HE COULD *BUY* THE MUSEUM SIX TIMES OVER.
NEWDAY

I THINK *YOU'RE* THE ONE'S PEELED THAT POOR BASTARD AND *WORE* HIM LIKE PAJAMAS!
I THINK *YOU'RE* THE ONE I'M LOOKING FOR!

10341
IF THAT IS TRUE, THEN THE MURDERS WILL *STOP.*
EXCEPT THEY *WON'T.*

THIS IS YOURS?
IT WILL BE WHEN IT'S FINISHED.
A LITTLE BIT OF PRE-COLUMBIAN MEXICO FOR THE 21ST CENTURY.
WILL IT BE OFFICES OR RESIDENTIAL?
OFFICES.
THOUGH I HAVE A COMPLETED SUITE OF ROOMS AT THE PEAK.
THE GRAND OPENING IS WEEKS AWAY.
AND YOU'RE EXPECTING ME TO GO UP TO YOUR ROOMS FOR A LITTLE BREAKFAST?
NOTHING LIKE THAT.

I'LL TREAT YOU TO THE FINEST BREAKFAST BURRITO IN SAN DIEGO.
HARDHATS MUST BE WORN/ LOS HARDHATS DEBEN SER GASTADOS

GOOD?
GOD, YES. THE CHORIZO IS AMAZING.
MAYBE WE ARE EVEN NOW, EH?

DEPENDS. WHY WERE THOSE GUYS TRYING TO KILL YOU?
AND DON'T GIVE ME THAT 'ROBBERY' B.S.

WHO KNOWS. WITH POWER COMES ENEMIES.
UNION ACTIVISTS? THE CARTELS? I HAVE MADE A HABIT OF NOT APPEASING THE CRIMINAL ELEMENT.

THAT'S JUST ANOTHER BRAND OF B.S., SEÑOR VILLARAIGOSA.
HA! HA!
CALL ME GERMÁN, PLEASE. OR GERRY.

PRINTS ARE BACK ON JORGE AND HIS AMIGO.
THE CLOWNS WHO SHOT AT VILLARAIGOSA?
YEAH.

EVER HEAR OF *LA LUZ DEL MUNDO?*
NO, JACK.
CHRISTIAN CULT BASED IN GUADALAJARA.
THE SHOOTERS WERE ***MEMBERS?***

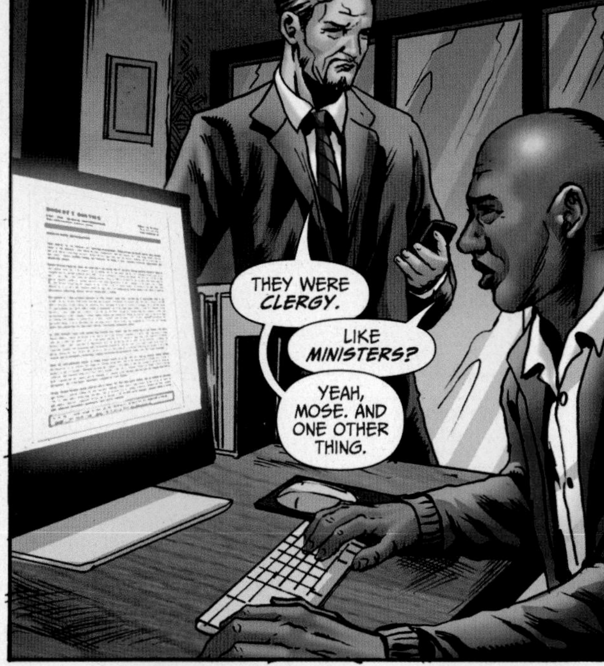
THEY WERE ***CLERGY.***
LIKE ***MINISTERS?***
YEAH, MOSE. AND ONE OTHER THING.

BORDER PATROL HAS THEM AT THE CROSSING STATION AT CHULA VISTA AT THE TIME OF THE MUSEUM MURDER.
DAMN!

WE NEED TO STEP ***LIGHTLY*** HERE, JACK.
WE SCREW UP, WE END UP CHECKING BEACH TAGS AT TORREY PINES.
NEWDAY

NOK NOK
UH?

I *GAVE* YOU A KEY, ROBYN!
OR DID YOU FORGET *THAT*, TOO?

OH!

AW, *DAMN!*

OKAY. *THIS* IS DIFFERENT.

THEY EVEN COVERED THE *CEILING* IN CROSSES.

WHAT'S IT *MEAN,* JACK?

IT MEANS, *SCREW* IT, I'M LIGHTING UP.

MARIAN!
YOU HAVE TO HAVE ONE OF THESE BURRITOS.

IS THAT SAM?
SHOULDN'T SHE BE IN THE HOSPITAL?
SHE CAME BACK A FEW HOURS AGO.

THERE'S NOTHING THEY CAN DO FOR HER, ROBYN. SHE'S BEYOND THE KIND OF HELP THEY CAN OFFER.
SO, THIS IS WITCHY STUFF?

YES. 'WITCHY' STUFF.
THIS GOWN STINKS LIKE LOW TIDE. AND ALL THIS BLOOD. WHERE THE HELL WAS SHE?
THAT'S WHAT I'M GOING TO FIND OUT.

STAY CLOSE, ROBYN.
I'VE NEVER TRIED THIS BEFORE.

DO YOU KNOW WHAT YOU'RE DOING?
NO. BUT I NEED TO REACH HER. I NEED TO KNOW WHAT'S HAPPENED.

SAM?
I AM HERE. AND I AM NOT HERE.
I AM THERE AND HERE.

WHERE IS 'THERE', SAM?

ACROSS THE GULF OF SPACE. STARS IN THE SKY I CANNOT NAME.
SEE IT THROUGH MY EYES. SEE IT THROUGH THE EYES OF MY HOST.

MARIAN...
SHOW ME, SAM. SHOW ME WHAT YOU SEE.

AHH!
MARIAN!

A GATEWAY IS OPEN THAT CANNOT BE CLOSED.
TO AN ANGRY PLACE. A VIOLENT PLACE.
A BILLION GALAXIES, DISTANT IN THE EVENT HORIZON OF A GRAVITY WELL.
THERE IS LIFE HERE. ANCIENT, MALEVOLENT AND POWERFUL.
AND HUNGRY.

HUNGRY...

WE WERE IDIOTS, ROBYN. PLAYING AT SOMETHING WE DIDN'T UNDERSTAND.
RELAX, MARIAN. IT WAS JUST A VISION.
NO!

IT'S REAL! HORRIBLY REAL!
AND NOW THERE'S A BRIDGE BETWEEN OUR WORLDS.

A BRIDGE? WHAT KIND OF BRIDGE?
HER. THE BRIDGE IS HER.

DID SOMEONE SAY SOMETHING ABOUT BURRITOS?
I'M STARVING.
TO BE CONTINUED

ROBYN HOOD

zenescope

3

DIXON
ABRERA
BEVARD
ESPOSITO

ROBYN HOOD

THE CURSE

DETENTION CENTER.
SAN DIEGO.

UH?

SOMEONE IS THERE?
SERÁS LIBERADO, AMIGO.

COMO LA MUERTE NOS LIBERA A TODOS, ¿NO?
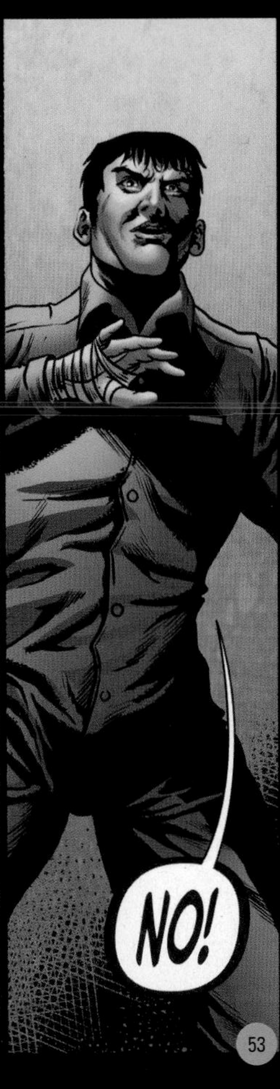
NO!

DEATH IS THE *ULTIMATE* RELEASE!
AND YOU MAY THANK **MY** GOD RATHER THAN YOURS!

SAM?
WHERE ARE YOU?

I KNOW YOU'RE HERE SOMEWHERE.
OH!

NO...

SAM!

SAM, HELP ME!

HELP YOU, MARIAN?

WHY WOULD I HELP YOU?
AN INSIGNIFICANT SPECK, A BACTERIUM, A PITIFUL COLLECTION OF CELLS.
AND WHAT PURPOSE WOULD THAT SERVE IN THE GRAND SCHEME OF THE UNIVERSE?
SAM!

SAM!
SAM?
RIGHT HERE, SWEETHEART.
WHO ELSE?
HAVE A NIGHTMARE?
I'M NOT SURE...
NO WONDER YOU CRASHED SO HARD AFTER THE SCARE I GAVE YOU, POOR THING.
I SAW YOU... BUT IT WASN'T YOU...
AND THE PLACE... NEVER BEEN THERE BEFORE...
WELL, IT IS ME AND THIS IS OUR PLACE.
ROBYN. WHERE'S ROBYN?
OFF WITH THAT BILLIONAIRE SHE PICKED UP.

"I THINK THE GIRL'S GOT IT *BAD* FOR THAT GUY."

FOR *ME?*

WHO ELSE?

YOU *SHOULDN'T* HAVE, GERRY.

WHAT AM I *LOOKING* AT HERE, JACK?
SURVEILLANCE VIDEO FROM THE COUNTY LOCK-UP LAST NIGHT.
WHEN SOMEONE TURNED OUR SUSPECT INTO A CANOE?
YEAH.

IT'S BART LESTER'S UNIT.
AND THAT'S BART LESTER.

WHAT'S GOING ON, JACK?
JORGE DIAZ'S CRAZY STORY? MAYBE NOT SO CRAZY.

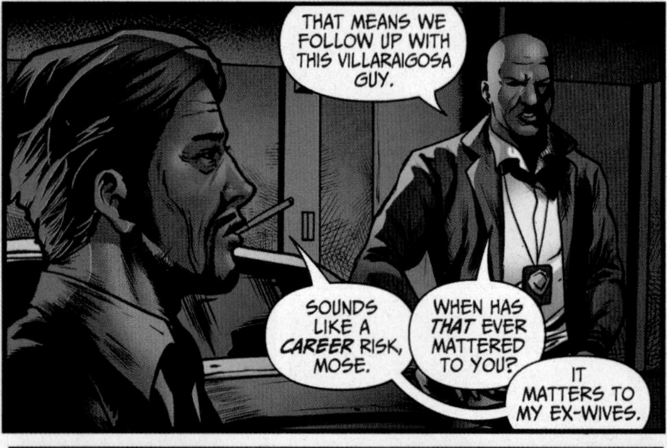

AMAZING, *CARA MIA*. THAT IS WHAT? EIGHT HUNDRED METERS? NINE?

CLOSER TO, LIKE, TWELVE HUNDRED. YOU'RE SURE THE TENANTS IN THAT BUILDING DON'T *MIND* ME SHOOTING AT THEM?

I AM THE *LANDLORD*. LET THEM *COMPLAIN*.

THEN KEEP WATCHING.

IMPRESSIVE.

¡ASOMBROSO!

HOW IS THAT *POSSIBLE?*
VISION MEMORY? TALENT? I TRY NOT TO *THINK* ABOUT IT.
YOU ARE A WOMAN OF MANY SURPRISES.

I *LIKE* A BIT OF MYSTERY, GERRY.
AS DO I.

YOU NEED TO HIT THE BRAKES, GERRY. WE *BOTH* DO.
I DON'T SEE WHY.
WELL, *I* DO.

I DON'T KNOW YOU. DON'T *REALLY* KNOW YOU.
AND I'M NOT *READY* TO BE IN THE KIND OF RELATIONSHIP YOU WANT.

EXCUSE ME, SEÑOR VILLARAIGOSA.
SÍ, HERNANDO?
THE PARTY PLANNERS ARE HERE.

A PARTY?
SOMETHING THAT HAS BEEN IN THE WORKS FOR *QUITE* A WHILE.
UN ESPECIAL EVENT.

SOME KIND OF MEXICAN HOLIDAY? A BUSINESS THING?
MORE PERSONAL. AN ANNIVERSARY OF SORTS.

I DO NOT WANT TO REVEAL THE THEME OF THE PARTY JUST YET, ROBYN. YOU ARE INVITED, OF COURSE.
A LOT OF BIG NAMES, HUH?
THE BIGGEST.

SO, A SURPRISE PARTY.
SÍ.
A SURPRISE FOR WHO?
EVERYONE.

OH, EXCUSE ME. YOU ARE THE PARTY PLANNERS?
NOT REALLY, SIR.

WE HAVE A FEW QUESTIONS FOR YOU.
THE LADY TOO, WHILE WE'RE AT IT.

MEXICANA AIR ONE-OH-SEVEN FROM VERA CRUZ.

ARE YOU HERE FOR BUSINESS OR PLEASURE, SEÑORS?
BUSINESS.
WE ARE THE BAND HERE TO PLAY AT A BIG PARTY FOR SEÑOR VILLARAIGOSA.
OKAY THEN.

AREN'T MARIACHI BANDS SUPPOSED TO LOOK HAPPY?
I DUNNO.

WHERE DID YOU GO?
I WAS GETTING CHILLY. NEED SOMETHING WITH SLEEVES.
WELL, IT'S TAKING YOU FOREVER, MARIAN.
I'M LOOKING FOR THAT PULLOVER I BOUGHT WHEN WE WERE IN LONDON.
I HOPE YOU DON'T THINK I'D EVER WEAR THAT HIDEOUS THING.
IT'S HERE SOMEWHERE.
BORED HERE. VERY BORED.
AMUSE YOURSELF. I'LL ONLY BE A MINUTE.
OH, I WILL.
COULD YOU COME IN HERE A MINUTE, SAM?
OKAY! OH-KAY!
YOU DIDN'T.

YOU ACTUALLY EXPECT THIS TO *WORK?*

HASTILY DONE, BUT EFFECTIVE. DEVIL OF A TIME DOING IT *QUIETLY.*

WHATEVER YOU ARE, IT WILL HOLD YOU.

SHE'S THERE. I CAN FEEL IT.
YOU ARE FEELING A MEMORY. ALL THAT IS SAM IS FAR, FAR FROM HERE.
YOUR LOVER LIVES NOW IN MY HOME, AND I IN HERS.
SHE WALKS IN MY PLACE DOWN SUNLESS CORRIDORS ON ALIEN LIMBS IN THE OLDEST PART OF THE CELESTIAL FIRMAMENT.
AN ENTIRELY COMPLETE ASTRAL TRANSFERAL? IMPOSSIBLE.
THERE'S SOMETHING OF SAM STILL HERE. A VESTIGE. THAT'S ALL I NEED.
THIS LOVE IS A THING FOR FOOLS.
WOULD YOU LIKE TO SEE WHAT SAM SEES?
THROUGH HER EYES?
I WOULD.
GAZE UPON IT. DO NOT TURN AWAY.
THIS IS THE PLACE WHERE YOUR SUMMONS WERE HEARD.
NO...

IS THIS WHERE I ASK FOR A LAWYER?
DO YOU WANT A LAWYER?
AM I UNDER ARREST?
DO YOU WANT TO BE UNDER ARREST?
ENOUGH WITH THIS ESTUPIDEZ! I AM NOT SOME PEON COME TO WASH YOUR CAR OR MOW YOUR LAWN!
I OWN THE RESTAURANTS YOU EAT IN! THE PLACES YOU PARK YOUR CAR! THE HOTELS WHERE YOU TAKE YOUR MISTRESS!
A MISTRESS? ON A COP'S SALARY? HELL, I DON'T EVEN HAVE CABLE.
WHAT DO YOU WANT FROM ME?
A FEW QUESTIONS.
LIKE WHY DOES SOME CHRISTIAN CULT HAVE SUCH A HARD-ON FOR YOU?
AND HOW DO YOU THINK ONE OF THEM GOT CHOPPED UP LIKE CARNE IN A CITY JAIL CELL?

DOING IN SAN DIEGO?
YOU KNOWN THIS GUY?
VISITING FRIENDS.
AND I DIDN'T KNOW GERRY UNTIL THAT NIGHT I SAVED HIS LIFE.
'GERRY,' HUH? I GUESS HIS MONEY MAKES HIM A CATCH.
I DON'T THINK IN TERMS LIKE THAT.
EVERYONE THINKS IN TERMS OF CASH.
I LIKE HIM.
OKAY. LOOKING PAST THAT.
YOU JUST HAPPENED TO BE CYCLING AROUND THE BAY WITH A COMPOUND BOW?
WITH CALIFORNIA'S GUN LAWS?
WHAT'S A POOR, DEFENSELESS, SINGLE GIRL TO DO?

MARIAN?

YOU HAVE TO *HELP* ME, MARIAN.
HM?

IT'S ME.
SAM?
YES, IT'S SAM.

I'M *FREE.* I'M *BACK* IN MY BODY.
PLEASE *RELEASE* ME. PLEASE, BEFORE THEY *TAKE* ME AGAIN.

I *CAN'T* GO BACK! THE THINGS THEY MAKE ME *DO*... PLEASE... MARIAN... PLEASE...

WHAT'S MY FAVORITE PIZZA TOPPING?

YOU...

...BITCH!

WOW!

DO YOU SEE THIS?
WEIRD.

BET THAT'S ONE OF THOSE LEGENDARY COMIC CON PARTIES.
WE SHOULD CRASH IT. I BET DOWNEY JR.'S UP THERE.

Park Ave
COME ON! WE NEED TO GO!
NOT GOING. TIRED. NEED SLEEP.
AWW!

I WILL FREE MYSELF.
SHUT UP, I'M READING.

THANKS FOR THE RIDE, OFFICERS.

AND A **WONDERFUL** EVENING OUT.

NOT MUCH OF A DATE.

I HAD FUN.

SERIOUSLY?

NO.

A TEXT FROM MY OFFICE.

THE TROUBLE OF DOING BUSINESS IN A **GLOBAL** ECONOMY.

A TWENTY-FOUR HOUR CLOCK.

YES. DO YOU MIND?

I CAN GET A CAR FOR YOU.

THAT'S OKAY. I'LL WALK. HERE'S HERNANDO WITH MY BOW.

<YOU HAVE NEED OF US, LORD VILLARAIGOSA?>*
*TRANSLATED FROM SPANISH.
<I WOULD NOT HAVE SUMMONED YOU OTHER-WISE.>
<THERE IS WORK TO DO. THE STARS AND PLANETS ALIGN. TWO NIGHTS FROM NOW, I WILL NEED YOU.>
<AND YOU MUST BE PROPERLY ATTIRED.>
<AS THE GABACHOS SAY-->
CLOTHES MAKE THE MAN.
TO BE CONTINUED

ROBYN HOOD

zenescope
4
ROBYN HOOD
DIXON
ABRERA
BEVARD
ESPOSITO
THE CURSE

SOME OF THESE PRONUNCIATIONS ARE GOING TO BE ROUGH.
ISN'T IT REALLY IMPORTANT TO GET THEM RIGHT?
IT IS.
ONE WONKY SYLLABLE AND WE COULD FIND OURSELVES ON THE BOTTOM OF THE SEA OR IN A ROOM FILLED WITH CARNIVOROUS MONKEYS.
WHERE IN THE WORLD DID YOU GET THIS BOOK ANYWAY?
I KNOW A GUY WHO KNOWS A GUY WHO KNOWS AN ANCIENT PERSIAN MAZZAKIM.
MARIAN, MAYBE THIS ISN'T SUCH A GREAT IDEA.
WHAT AM I SUPPOSED TO DO, ROBYN? LEAVE SAM THE WAY SHE IS?

LEAVE HER LIKE--
--THIS?
...YOUR DEATHS WILL LAST AN ETERNITY...

N'GRATHL RZI MORLENNDA---NO, MOR-LENT-UH, SUGGOTH RZI N'ITHWRA...

...YOU WILL SCREAM IN AGONY FOR MILLENNIA...

IZ'NHULL RZI B'RTHALLZUH GUH N'TH'RHVEENU YOG RZI MET'HNOOR.
MARIAN.

MARIAN, WHY ARE YOU DOING THIS TO ME?

S'S'NIGHTHRA NUHHMA RZE ALL'GHODAR ZBN RALL-UL-DEETH'RA.

I AM WARNING YOU. PROCEED NO FURTHER AND I WILL MAKE YOUR DEATHS QUICK ONES.

B'RTH'SH'LAH MOG'OHH R'HENN!
YAAAAGH!

THAT'S IT? IT'S OVER?
IT'S A BEGINNING.
IS SHE... DEAD?

NO. SHE'S COMATOSE AGAIN.
BRAIN DEAD THEN?
MORE LIKE SOUL DEAD.

I'VE RIDDED HER BODY OF THE PRESENCE THAT WAS POSSESSING HER. BUT HER ESSENCES, HER PSYCHE, IS STILL SOMEWHERE ON THE OTHER SIDE OF THE UNIVERSE.
WHAT WE'RE LOOKING AT IS AN EMPTY SHELL.

SO...
WHAT'S GOING ON WITH YOU?

THESE TWO THREATEN ALL I HAVE CREATED HERE.
THEY MUST DIE. *TONIGHT.*
"THE PHONE WILL TAKE YOU TO WHERE THEY WORK. YOU WILL HUNT. YOU WILL WATCH.
"AND WHEN YOU *SEE* THEM, YOU WILL KILL."
WE'RE GETTING NOWHERE FAST HERE, JACK.
WE'RE GETTING NOWHERE, *PERIOD.*
WE ARE *OFF* THIS CASE.

THE MAYOR CRAPS ON THE DEPUTY MAYOR WHO CRAPS ON THE POLICE CHIEF WHO CRAPPED ON US.
GUESS WE'RE LUCKY WE STILL HAVE OUR SHIELDS.
PULLING IN A MEXICAN BILLIONAIRE AND HIS CHIPPIE FOR QUESTIONING WAS A BONEHEAD MOVE.
I STILL SAY THAT VILLARAIGOSA'S CONNECTED TO ALL THIS. MAYBE THE GIRL, TOO.
THAT'S ALL FOR SOMEONE ELSE TO WORK OUT.
YEAH. WHILE THE BODIES PILE UP.
LEAVE IT BE, MOSE. WALK AWAY.
I'M GOIN' BACK INSIDE. YOU COMING?
I'LL BE ALONG.
135-P
THOSE THINGS'LL KILL YOU.
MM.

WHAT IN--
JACK?
MOSE!
JACK!
WHAT ARE THEY WEARING?
POK
UNH!

SON OF A BITCH!
POOM
CHOOM
OFFICER DOWN! OFFICER DOWN! REAR LOT!
SUSPECTS FLEEING TOWARD THE PARK!
WHAT THE HELL ARE THEY WEARING?

TELL ME ABOUT THIS *GUY.*
WITH EVERYTHING *YOU* HAVE GOING ON RIGHT NOW?
YOU DON'T NEED TO HEAR MY SOAP OPERA.
TELL ME.
HAVE YOU BEEN FOOD SHOPPING THIS *YEAR?*

DOES MY LOVE LIFE AMUSE YOU?
SORRY. I'M A LITTLE PUNCHY.
I TOLD YOU.
TOLD ME WHAT?
THAT MY WORRIES ARE PIDDLY COMPARED TO HAVING THE LOVE OF YOUR LIFE SUCKED INTO A DARK UNIVERSE AND REPLACED WITH A MALIGNANT ALIEN PRESENCE.
WHEN YOU PUT IT THAT WAY, IT SOUNDS WEIRD.
HELL. IT IS WEIRD.
LOOK, WHY DON'T YOU LET ME MEET THIS AWESOME GUY?
WHY?
I'M A WITCH, REMEMBER? I CAN GET A READ OFF HIM.
SEEMS LIKE CHEATING.
IT DOES, RIGHT?
WHAT ABOUT SAM?
WE WON'T BE GONE THAT LONG. AND I HAVE GOT TO GET OUT OF HERE AWHILE.
CLEAR MY HEAD. GET MY THOUGHTS TOGETHER.

I'LL GET US AN UBER.
ARE YOU SURE?
SAM WILL BE FINE. WELL, NOT 'FINE'--
"--BUT SHE'S NOT GOING ANYWHERE WITH ALL THE WARDING SIGNS I POSTED."

WE *COULD* HAVE TAKEN MY CYCLE.
I *HATE* WHAT A HELMET DOES TO MY HAIR.
AND I'D *LIKE* TO ARRIVE IN ONE PIECE.
SAYS THE SAME GIRL WHO MESSES WITH DARK MAGIC LIKE OTHER PEOPLE PLAY ANGRY BIRDS.
THIS IS WHERE THIS GUY LIVES?
YOU SAID HE HAD MONEY.
BUT THIS IS *MON*-NAY!
YOU TWO! ***STOP!***

THIS IS A *HARD HAT* AREA, LADIES.
WELL, THANK YOU *SO* MUCH.

THOUGHT YOU *HATED* WHAT HELMETS DO TO YOUR HAIR.
SHUT *UP*, ROBYN.

MS. LOCKSLEY? POLICE.
DETECTIVE SERGEANT WILLIAMS. OPEN UP, PLEASE.
SCREW THIS.
KRAK
I'LL LET MYSELF IN.
I HOPE THIS ADDRESS YOU GAVE US IS RIGHTEOUS, MS. LOCKSLEY.
HATE TO THINK YOU LIED TO ME AND MY PARTNER.
MY DEAD PARTNER. OR MAYBE YOU ALREADY KNEW THAT. HUH, MS.--
--THE HELL?

THIS IS WILLIAMS. I NEED AN *AMBULANCE* TO SEVEN-THREE-SEVEN BALBOA. APARTMENT THREE-OH SEVEN.

AND SEND SOME *UNIFORMS* TOO. YEAH, A *HOMICIDE.*

I WASN'T *EXPECTING* YOU, CARA MIA.

YOU DID NOT CALL.

NO...

MARIAN?
S'OKAY. JUST SICK ALL OF A SUDDEN.

I'M SORRY, GERMÁN. I--
SEE TO YOUR *AMIGA*. I AM CERTAIN SHE WILL RECOVER.

WHAT'S WRONG? WHAT WAS THAT?
WHEN I TOUCHED HIS HAND...

YOU HAVE TO *PROMISE* ME TO STAY AWAY FROM HIM.
YOU *READ* HIM? IT'S *THAT* BAD?
TRUST ME, GIRLFRIEND--

--IT DOESN'T *GET* WORSE.

WHAT DID YOU SEE?
MAYBE IT WAS IMAGES FROM HIS THOUGHTS. OR MEMORIES. OR A PREMONITION.

IT WAS REAL. AS REAL AS YOU AND I SITTING HERE.
I SAW BLOOD. I SAW FEAR. I SAW DEATH. LOTS OF DEATH.

NOW WHAT?

HOLD ON! WHERE ARE YOU TAKING HER?

MS. LOCKSLEY, YOU HAVE THE RIGHT TO REMAIN SILENT...

WHAT'S THIS ABOUT?
I'M ARRESTING HER FOR ATTEMPTED MURDER.
ROBYN DIDN'T DO THIS! I DID!

FINE. YOU'RE BOTH UNDER ARREST.
HAPPY NOW?

THIS ISN'T GOOD.

I THOUGHT YOU SAID SAM WAS OKAY WHILE YOUR SPELL HELD HER.

ONLY WHEN SHE'S INSIDE THE WARDING CIRCLE. THAT STUPID COP FREED HER.
I HAVE NO CONTROL OVER WHAT--
UH. UH. UH.

OH.

THIS IS YOUR LUCKY NIGHT, LADIES.
YOU'RE BEING CUT LOOSE.
ALL CHARGES DROPPED, WILLIAMS?
YEAH. YEAH. THE DOCS LOOKED OVER YOUR LITTLE FRIEND.
NO SIGN OF INJURY OR ABUSE. TOX SCREEN CAME BACK CLEAN. WHATEVER WEIRD CRAP YOU TWO ARE INTO DIDN'T HARM HER.
THEY CAN'T FIGURE OUT WHAT'S GOING ON WITH HER.
YOU HAD NO RIGHT TO TAKE HER.
THAT'S NOT HOW IT LOOKED TO ME.
WHERE'S SAM NOW?
SHE'S BEEN TAKEN TO KAISER.
I'LL DRIVE YOU OVER THERE. MY WAY OF APOLOGIZING.

"AND THESE READINGS ARE *ACCURATE?*"

"YES, DOCTOR."

THESE *CT* SCANS CONTRADICT THE EEG.

THAT'S WHY THE CHIEF SURGEON WANTED SOMEONE FROM *NEURO* TO LOOK AT HER.

THE ONLY *POSSIBLE* CONCLUSIONS ARE EITHER A MALFUNCTION IN THE EQUIPMENT, OR THIS PATIENT IS FAKING A COMA.

HOW DO YOU *FAKE* A COMA, DOCTOR?

IT'S *POSSIBLE.* LET'S SEE IF SHE RESPONDS TO STIMULI.

I CAN *TRY* AN IV NEEDLE IN HER--

AAAHHH!

GAS STATION
I HOPE YOUR FRIEND IS ALL RIGHT.
SAM'S TOUGH. SHE'LL PULL THROUGH.
TOUGH, *HUH?* BUT ***STRANGE,*** RIGHT?
MEANING?
SHE'S INTO SOME ***WEIRD*** STUFF.
I FOUND HER LAYING IN A ***CIRCLE*** OF DEAD ANIMALS. RATS. MICE. ROACHES. SPIDERS.
LOOKED LIKE ***VOODOO*** CRAP. WHAT DO ***YOU*** KNOW ABOUT THAT?
SHE WAS INTO HOLISTIC HEALING.
NOT THE ***CRAZIEST*** THING I'VE SEEN THIS WEEK.
MY ***PARTNER*** WAS KILLED BY SOME FREAKS DRESSED IN HUMAN SKINS.
YOU ***BELIEVE*** THAT CRAP?
WHAT KIND OF SKINS?

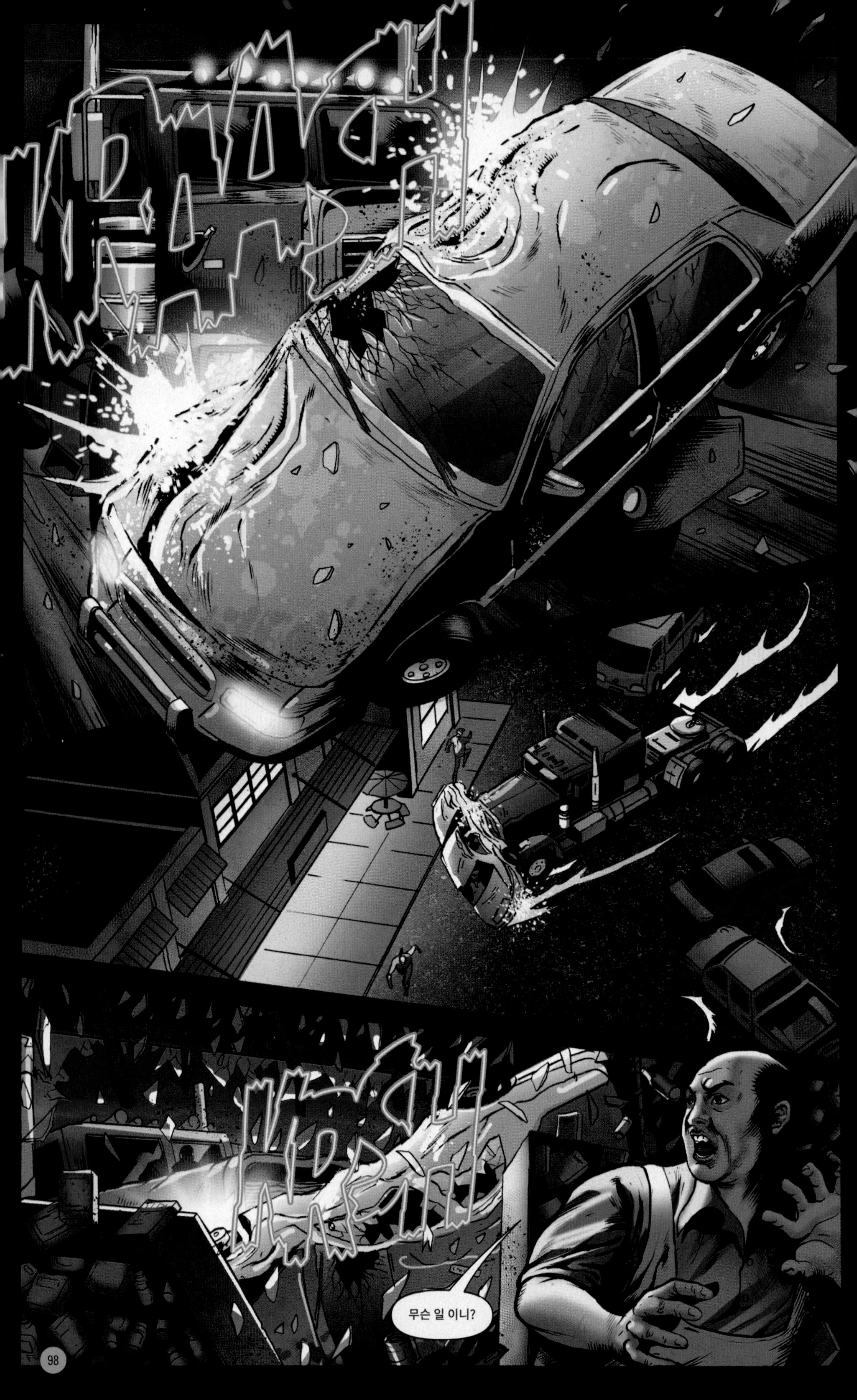
무슨 일 이니?

FREE WIFI
ROBBED TWICE THIS YEAR!
NO MORE!
너 누구 니?
ROBYN, WAKE UP!
YOU HAVE TO WAKE UP!
TO BE CONTINUED

zenescope
ROBYN HOOD
5
DIXON
ABRERA
BEVARD
ESPOSITO
THE CURSE
CHEN

MOSE!
I NEED YOU TO WAKE UP NOW!

I LEFT MY *BOW* AT MARIAN'S!

AND WE HAVE A *LAW ENFORCEMENT* SITUATION HERE!

AAH!
ICUATIATETEC CIHUAPILI!
IS THAT A PERSON YOU'RE WEARING?
AXNOHTIC ICHPUCATI!
NNGH!
SICK!
KRK

CHICAHTIC
CIHUAOILI!

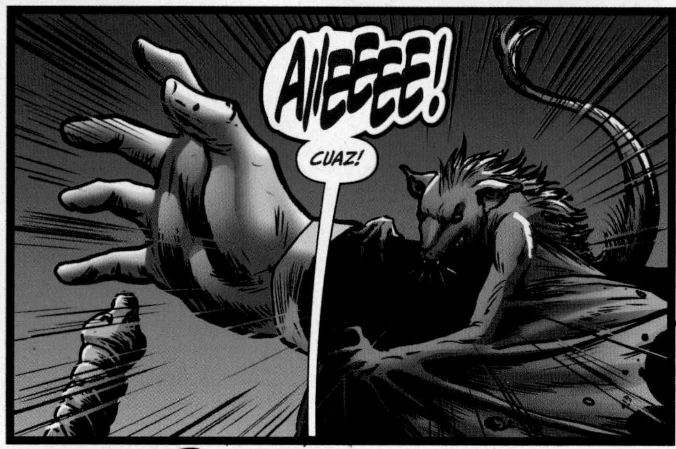

ROBYN!

I SEE HIM!
ICHPUCATI!
THE OTHER ONE CALLED ME THAT!

SOUNDS NASTY!

AXNOHTIC CIHUAPILI!
YOU TOO, BUDDY.

CHOOM

WHAT'D I MISS?
EVERYTHING.

TWO DEAD PERPS. AND IT LOOKS LIKE YOU USED MY WEAPON.
THE PAPERWORK'S GONNA BE UNFORGIVING.

THIS IS ON ME. GET OUT OF HERE.
MOSE...
GO!

I FEEL BAD LEAVING HIM.
YOU WANT TO STAY WHILE THEY ASK A BUNCH OF QUESTIONS WE CAN'T ANSWER?
NOT REALLY.
GOOD. WE HAVE BETTER THINGS TO DO--

"--LIKE KEEPING AN EYE ON YOUR CREEPY BOYFRIEND."
IT IS A VERY SPECIAL NIGHT. YOU MIGHT SAY THE KIND OF NIGHT THAT ONLY COMES ONCE IN A THOUSAND YEARS.
YOU'RE PROMISING A BIG SURPRISE TONIGHT, SEÑOR VILLARAIGOSA.

MORE LIKE A REVELATION. I ASSURE YOU THAT THE WORLD WILL NEVER BE THE SAME.
INTRIGUING. IS IT A TECHNOLOGY ROLL-OUT?
NOTHING SO ORDINARY, CARRIE.

IT IS CLOSER TO A SPIRITUAL EXISTENCE.
I DO NOT EXAGGERATE WHEN I SAY THAT NO ONE WHO SEES THIS WILL EVER LOOK AT THE WORLD THE SAME WAY.

LIVE
YOU DON'T WANT TO MISS THIS.
YOU SEEING THIS?
CELEB BASH IN SAN DIEGO

WHATEVER YOUR BOYFRIEND'S UP TO, IT'S JUMPING OFF NOW.
HE'S NOT MY BOYFRIEND, MARIAN.

*REAL*ISTIC.
AND WHAT ABOUT SAM? SHE'S ON THE LOOSE.
SAM?

MA'AM? MISS?

COULD YOU STEP BACK FROM THE LEDGE, MA'AM?
WE'LL TAKE YOU BACK TO YOUR ROOM, OKAY?

OR WHEREVER YOU WANT TO GO. WHERE DO YOU WANT TO GO?
HOME.

I'M GOING HOME.

NOT ON *THIS* ROAD.

HANG ON--

OH!

--WE'RE USING AN *ALTERNATE* ROUTE.

ROBYN!

WELCOME TO THE SEASON'S PRIMO EVENT--THE GRAND OPENING OF THE VILLARAIGOSA CENTER!
EVERYBODY WHO'S ANYBODY IS PILING OUT OF LIMOS AND UBERS AND LYFTS TO SEE AND BE SEEN AT THE BILLIONAIRE'S MEGA-MEGA SUPER PARTY!

BRIGHAM PRATT, STAR OF THE NEW FAST AND FABULOUS MOVIE--WHAT BRINGS YOU HERE TONIGHT?
STRICTLY FOR CHARITY, LACEY. I TRY TO HELP OUT WHENEVER AND WHEREVER I CAN.
TELL US MORE ABOUT THE CAUSE YOU'RE HERE TO RAISE MONEY FOR.

IT'S FOR THE KIDS, RIGHT? OR CANCER RESEARCH?
SOMETHING TO DO WITH STRAY PETS?
THE HOMELESS?

IDIOTS.

THEY COME WILLINGLY. THEY COME LAUGHING.
LITTLE KNOWING THEIR WORLD IS DRAWING TO A CLOSE.

WHY DIDN'T YOU WAIT UNTIL THE LAST DAY OF THE CON TO BUY THIS?
UGH!
IT WOULDA BEEN GONE!
IG!

AND HAVE YOU THOUGHT OF HOW YOU'RE GONNA GET THIS HOME?
I'LL FED-EX IT!
AND YOUR MOM'S GONNA RAGE WHEN SHE SEES IT!
SHE DOESN'T TELL ME WHAT TO DO!

WHOA.
HOT COSPLAY, GIRL!

THANKS.
YOU TOO.

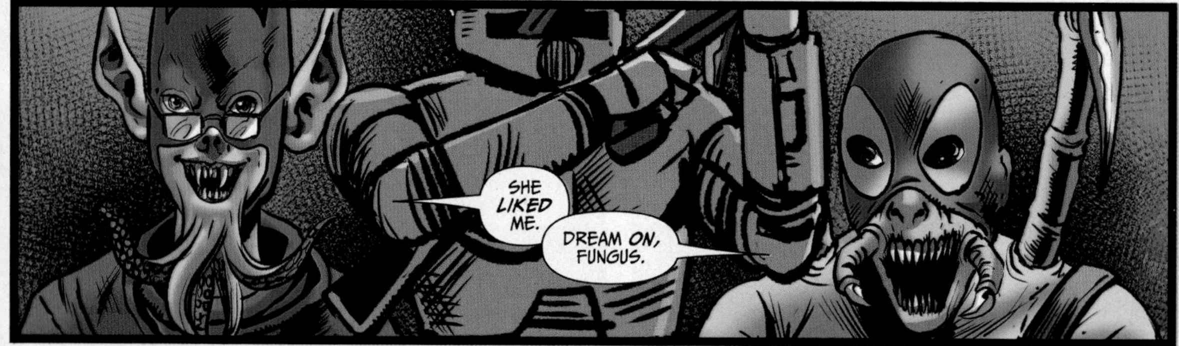

SHE LIKED ME.
DREAM ON, FUNGUS.

YAAAAAAH!
LOOKIT YOU!
LOOK AT YOU!

THIS IS AS CLOSE AS WE *GET* ON WHEELS.
HUH?
WE CAN GO THE *REST* OF THE WAY ON FOOT.
THAT'S THE BEST NEWS I'VE HAD ALL *NIGHT*.

WE HAVING A GOOD TIME?
YEEEEAAHHH!

Y'KNOW THERE'S A METHOD TO THIS MADNESS!
A REASON FOR THE SEASON, A'IGHT!

SO LET ME BRING YOU THE MAN, THE HOMBRE, WHO MADE THIS PARTY HAPPEN!
HE'S A BILLIONAIRE WHO REALLY CARES! HE'S YOUR HOST--

GERRRRMÁN VILLARAIGOOOOOOSA!
HOLA, SAN DIEGO!

THANK YOU FOR JOINING ME ON THIS SPECIAL NIGHT!
AND IT IS A VERY SPECIAL NIGHT!

THE STARS AND PLANETS HAVE NOT BEEN SO ALIGNED FOR OVER TEN THOUSAND YEARS!
THIS PLACE, THIS CITY, IS AT THE FOCAL POINT OF ENERGY FROM THE OTHER SIDE OF THE UNIVERSE!

IT IS TIME TO SHED THIS MODERNISM, THIS WORLD OF EMPTY TECHNOLOGY AND HOLLOW JOY!
WITH YOUR HELP, TONIGHT, WE WILL ALL ENTER A NEW AGE!

WILL YOU HELP ME?
ME?
SÍ. YOU. WILL YOU BE THE FIRST OF MANY?

THIS ISN'T GOING TO HURT, IS IT?
YOU WILL NEVER REGRET IT.
IT WILL BE AN EXPERIENCE LIKE NO OTHER.

ALL RIGHT! I'M PLAYING ALONG, OKAY?
THECATL TLAHUIZCALPANTECHUHTLI KUKULKAN...

MIXCOATL Y XOCHIQUETZAL Y XOLOTL... XIQUIHTA!
NOCNEHUAN! NOPILHUAN! XIQUIHTA!

HEY, IS THIS LIKE A MAGIC ACT?
ARE YOU GONNA PULL A SNAKE FROM SOMEWHERE?

TLACAME... CHIHUAME... TATZINTL... XIQUIHTA!
PAPAQIZQUE!

OH.
WHAT?
WE MIGHT BE TOO LATE.

XIQUIHTA... XIQUIHTA...
QUETZALCOATL!

PLEASE TELL ME YOU'RE ON THE WAY.
I'M HEADING YOUR WAY WITH EVERYTHING I COULD GET MOBILZED.
YOU BETTER BE **RIGHT** ABOUT THIS, MS. LOCKSLEY. I CALLED IN EVERY FAVOR AND THEN SOME.
I ONLY HOPE IT'S ENOUGH. BELIEVE ME WHEN I SAY THIS--
--NO ONE'S **EVER** SEEN ANYTHING LIKE THIS BEFORE. NOT EVEN IN **CALIFORNIA**.
OH, ROBYN...
IT BETTER BE BIBLICAL, MS. LOCKSLEY. IT BETTER BE HUGER THAN HUGE. 'CAUSE LIKE I TOLD YOU--
--I **HATE** PAPERWORK!

WHOA! THAT LOOKS REAL!
THEY CAN DO ANYTHING WITH EFFECTS NOW.
YOU HEAR THAT CHICK SCREAM?
SHE'S STOPPED NOW.

NO CLEAR SHOT THROUGH ALL THESE PEOPLE!
WE HAVE TO GET CLOSER!
HE CAN'T BE ALLOWED TO COMPLETE THE INVOCATION!

OH YEAH, THIS IS GOING UP ON MY PAGE.
SOMETHING DOESN'T FEEL RIGHT, TREVOR.
WHAT? IT'S JUST A SHOW.

IS IT?

‹YOU HAVE OUR INVITATION!›*

‹YOU HAVE OUR OFFERING!›

‹WE HAVE INVOKED YOUR MANY NAMES!›

*TRANSLATED FROM NAHUATL, THE LANGUAGE OF THE AZTECS.

‹OPEN YOUR EYES TO SEE FOR THE FIRST TIME IN YOUR LIVES!›
‹OPEN YOUR MINDS TO UNDERSTAND THE UNTHINKABLE!›
BUM-
BUH-

BUM-
BUH-
‹HE COMES!›
‹HE COMES!›

HOW'RE THEY DOING THAT?
I DON'T KNOW!
SOMETHING'S WRONG HERE.
UM... ANYONE REMEMBER WHERE I PARKED THE CAR?

TO YOUR KNEES! BOW IN HIS PRESENCE!
YOUR WORLD ENDS NOW ONLY TO BE RE-BORN!
BUH-
BUM-
BUH-
BUM-

HE IS RETURNED!
THE FEATHERED SERPENT!
QUETZALCOATL--
--THE BIG Q!
TO BE CONCLUDED

ROBYN HOOD

zenescope
ROBYN HOOD
THE CURSE
6
DIXON
ABRERA
BEVARD
ESPOSITO

WELCOME, QUETZALCOATL!
YOU ARE BACK WHERE YOU BELONG TO RULE US ALL!

YES!
¡SÍ!
IT IS *I*, YOUR FAITHFUL ACOLYTE WHO BROUGHT YOU HERE!

THE CITY IS YOURS!
THE WORLD IS YOURS!
I GIVE IT TO YOU!

HUGE.

YOU ONCE TOLD ME THAT SIZE DOESN'T *MATTER* WHEN IT COMES TO MAGIC.

I *KNOW* I DID, BUT *LOOK* AT IT!

DO WHAT YOU *CAN,* MARIAN.

I'M GOING TO SEE IF I CAN HELP THAT IDIOT *GERMÁN.*

¿QUE?
GRACIAS, MY LORD!
YOU GIVE ME THE GIFT OF FLIGHT!
HAHA HAHAHAHAHAHA!

IF THERE'S ANYTHING YOU CAN DO, DO IT *NOW!*

THERE'S A *SPELL* I COULD TRY.

TRY IT!

WHERE WILL *YOU* BE?

RIGHT HERE. DOING THE ONLY THING I *CAN* DO.

MAN!

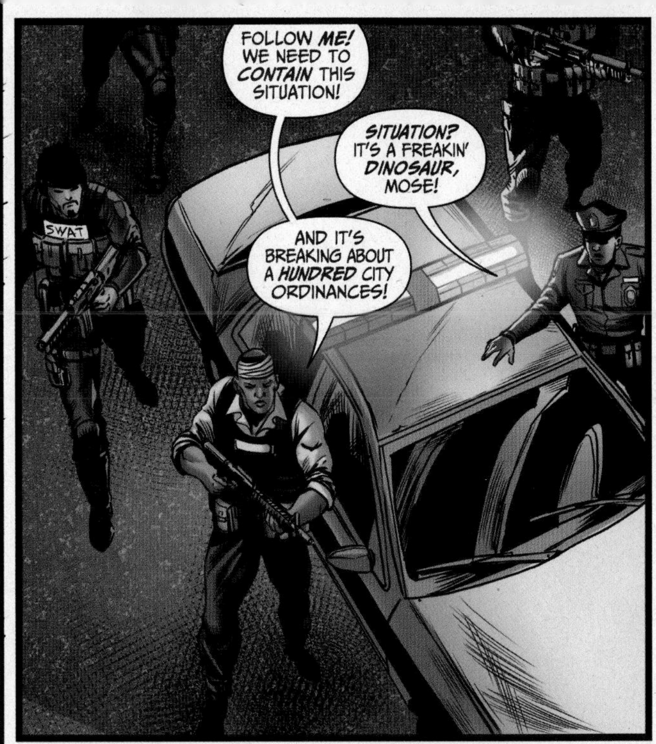
FOLLOW ME! WE NEED TO CONTAIN THIS SITUATION!
SITUATION? IT'S A FREAKIN' DINOSAUR, MOSE!
AND IT'S BREAKING ABOUT A HUNDRED CITY ORDINANCES!
SWAT

MISS!
YOU NEED TO GET OUT OF HERE!

HE'S RIGHT, YOU KNOW.

SAM.
THERE'S NOTHING BUT DANGER HERE FOR YOU.
DANGER BEYOND YOUR ABILITY TO UNDERSTAND.

FREE FIRE ZONE, GUYS AND GALS!
WHAT THE HELL ARE WE *DOING* HERE?
WHAT'S IT *SAY* ON THE SIDE OF OUR UNITS, ORTIZ?

POOM
POOM POOM
POOM
POOM
POOM
POOM
PROTECT AND SERVE!
POOM
POOM
POOM

POK
POK
POK
POK
POK
POK
POK
POK
POK
POK

UNNH!

TWO-BAKER-EIGHT TO BASE!
GO FOR BASE, BAKER.
SEND MORE UNITS! SEND THE ARMY! SEND THE MARINES!
SEND THE SEALS!

YOUR SKILLS ARE TOO WEAK TO AFFECT THE OUTCOME OF THIS NIGHT.
YOU ARE A LEAF IN A MAELSTROM.

THAT'S NOT TRUE!
PART OF HER IS HERE! I FEEL IT!

A VESTIGE PERHAPS.
YOU SHOULD KNOW THAT SHE LOVES YOU STILL. TOUCHING, REALLY. SUCH DEVOTION.

WHAT DO YOU WANT HERE?
WHY DON'T YOU GO BACK TO YOUR DARK CORNER OF THE UNIVERSE AND SET SAM FREE?

THAT'S WHY I'M HERE.
THIS PLACE BORES ME.

I WILL FIND MY WAY HOME.

BUT YOU WILL NEVER SEE YOUR LOVE AGAIN.

HUNH!
KRSSH
WOO!
WORK YOUR MOJO, MARIAN.
THERE'S ONLY SO MUCH TIME I CAN BUY--
--YOU!

CAN'T STOP YOU. CAN'T KILL YOU.
BUT I KNOW WHERE TO HURT YOU.
SHUNK
SOMETHING'S GOT IT PISSED OFF NOW!
WHOOSSH
NOW?
YOU MEAN IT'S JUST GETTING PISSED?

LADY... MA'AM..

YOU *DON'T* WANT TO BE HERE.

HAMMER ONE LEADER TO CORONADO!
GO FOR CORONADO, HAMMER ONE.
WE ARE OVER TARGET ZONE!
WE ARE TO ENGAGE A GIANT MONSTER IN DOWNTOWN SAN DIEGO?
ROGER THAT, HAMMER ONE.
REQUESTING FURTHER CLARIFICATION, CORONADO--

--WHICH GIANT MONSTER?

PH'NGLUI MGLW'NAFH C'RUTHU R'LYEH WGAH'NAGL FHTAGN.

THIS THING IS EVERYWHERE AT ONCE!
THIS ONE'S FOR *YOU*, BLINKY.
SKRSH
MUST BE ABLE TO *SMELL* ME.
COME *ON*, MARIAN!
MAKE ALL THIS GO *AWAY!*

KRSH
SKRAA
KRRN
KROOM
RHEEE

LOOKS LIKE THE UGLIER ONE IS WINNING.
AND WE LOSE EITHER WAY.

SKREE

O'LU'GHTH KAH'LAR'JAMA, JAME KAH'LARRA DIN. DIN O'LU N'GTHAR C'RUTHU.

--KAK

PH'NGLUI MGLW'NAFH NH'GAAL!

PI'THRA NH'GAAL! NH'GAAL!

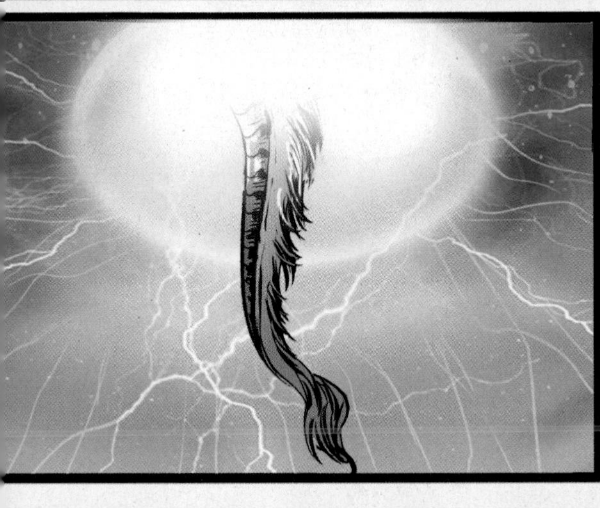

NH'GAAL!
NH'GAAL!

GONE.
JUST LIKE *THAT*. LIKE THEY NEVER *WERE*.

DO YOU THINK I'LL EVER SEE SAM AGAIN?

I KNOW HOW MUCH SHE **MEANS** TO YOU, MARIAN--

--BUT I HOPE TO HELL **NOT**.

THE END

ROBYN HOOD: THE CURSE 1 • COVER A

Artwork by Igor Vitorino • Colors by Kyle Ritter

ROBYN HOOD: THE CURSE 1 • COVER B

Artwork by Fritz Casas • Colors by Hedwin Zaldivar

ROBYN HOOD: THE CURSE 1 • COVER C
Artwork by Keith Garvey

ROBYN HOOD: THE CURSE 1 • COVER D

Artwork by Anthony Spay • Colors by Jorge Cortes

ROBYN HOOD: THE CURSE 1 • COVER E

Artwork by Leonardo Colapietro

ROBYN HOOD: THE CURSE 2 • COVER A

Artwork by Sheldon Goh • Colors by Sanju Nivangune

ROBYN HOOD: THE CURSE 2 • COVER B

Artwork by Julius Abrera • Colors by Ceci de la Cruz

ROBYN HOOD: THE CURSE 2 • COVER C

Artwork by Vincenzo Federici • Colors by Sanju Nivangune

ROBYN HOOD: THE CURSE 2 • COVER D

Artwork by Caanan White • Colors by Hedwin Zaldivar

ROBYN HOOD: THE CURSE 3 • COVER A
Artwork by Riveiro • Colors by Ceci de la Cruz

ROBYN HOOD: THE CURSE 3 • COVER B
Artwork by Julius Abrera • Colors by Robby Bevard

ROBYN HOOD: THE CURSE 3 • COVER C

Artwork by Noah Salonga • Colors by Ylenia Di Napoli

ROBYN HOOD: THE CURSE 3 • COVER D

Artwork by Sheldon Goh • Colors by Sanju NIvangune

ROBYN HOOD: THE CURSE 4 • COVER A

Artwork by Sergio Davila • Colors by Ceci de la Cruz

ROBYN HOOD: THE CURSE 4 • COVER B

Artwork by Mike S. Miller • Colors by Jorge Cortes

ROBYN HOOD: THE CURSE 4 • COVER C
Artwork by Jay Anacleto • Colors by Ula Mos

ROBYN HOOD: THE CURSE 4 • COVER D

Artwork by Caanan White • Colors by Hedwin Zaldivar

ROBYN HOOD: THE CURSE 5 • COVER A

Artwork by Sean Chen • Colors by Ivan Nunes

ROBYN HOOD: THE CURSE 5 • COVER B

Artwork by Anthony Spay • Colors by Grostieta

ROBYN HOOD: THE CURSE 5 • COVER C
Artwork by Kevin McCoy • Colors by Ula Mos

ROBYN HOOD: THE CURSE 5 • COVER D

Artwork by Julius Abrera • Colors by Hedwin Zaldivar

ROBYN HOOD: THE CURSE 6 • COVER A

Artwork by Riveiro • Colors by Ceci de la Cruz

ROBYN HOOD: THE CURSE 6 • COVER B

Artwork by Julius Abrera • Colors by Grostieta

ROBYN HOOD: THE CURSE 6 • COVER C

Artwork by Derlis Santacruz • Colors by Ula Mos

ROBYN HOOD: THE CURSE 6 • COVER D

Artwork by Harvey Tolibao • Colors by Ivan Nunes

zenescope

Van Helsing vs. Robyn Hood

Sneak Preview

TEDESCO · OTERO · PACIAROTTI · ESPOSITO

WRITER
RALPH
TEDESCO
ARTWORK
ALLAN
OTERO
COLORS
LEONARDO
PACIAROTTI
LETTERS
TAYLOR
ESPOSITO
(OF GHOST
GLYPH STUDIOS)
EDITOR
TERRY
KAVANAGH
COVER ART
SEAN
CHEN
IVAN
NUNES
KRAK
FAKE ACCENT? I'VE CLEARLY BEEN IN THE STATES TOO LONG.

UGNF!
ROBYN?

LIESEL! SERIOUSLY?
I'M SO SORRY, LOVE. OH MY GOD!
IT'S BEEN SO LONG.
I HAVEN'T BEEN ABLE TO GET IN TOUCH--
I WAS OFF THE GRID FOR A BIT. I ALSO HAD TO GET SMARTER ABOUT HOW I MEET CLIENTS, SO I CHANGED UP MY OPERATION.
BUT WE CAN FINISH CATCHING UP LATER. I GOTTA THINK YOU'RE HERE FOR THE SAME REASON I AM.
THE NAME VON RING ANY BELLS?
YEAH. MY CLIENT'S SON WENT MISSING A FEW WEEKS AGO. APPARENTLY HE WORKS FOR THE GUY.
TO BE CONTINUED IN
VAN HELSING VS. ROBYN HOOD
PAPERBACK AVAILABLE NOW!

ROBYN HOOD TRILOGY (2012)

Pat Shand (W) Larry Watts (A) Slamet Mujiono (C)

Inside the realm of Myst, a tyrant rules the city of Bree with an iron fist, leaving its citizens living in terror. But all hope is not lost as an orphaned teen from our world discovers her true destiny and becomes the legend she was meant to be.

ORIGIN ISBN: 978-1937068790
WANTED ISBN: 978-1939683045
LEGEND ISBN: 978-1939683885

"The most bad ass archer in comics..."
—Word of the Nerd

ROBYN HOOD: RIOT GIRLS SERIES (2014)

Pat Shand (W) Roberta Ingranata (A) Slamet Mujiono (C)

From drug lords, to corrupt politicians, to the things that go bump in the night, no evils that plague the streets of New York City will be safe as Robyn Locksley sets up shop as a private investigator. Joined by her best friend Marian Quin, a powerful witch from Myst, it's a whole new world for Robyn.

RIOT GIRLS ISBN: 978-1939683991
MONSTERS IN THE DARK ISBN: 978-1942275077
ATTITUDE ADJUSTMENT ISBN: 978-1942275152
UPRISING ISBN: 978-1942275312

ROBYN HOOD: I LOVE NY (2016)

Lou Iovino (W) Sergio Ariño (A) Grostieta (C)

This is the story of what comes next. It's the story of Robyn on her own for the first time, making her way toward an uncertain future. But most importantly, it's the story of a growing love affair between this unlikely outlaw hero and the greatest city on Earth, New York City—and how it saves them both.

ISBN: 978-1942275565

"*Robyn Hood: I Love NY* is a marvelous new beginning."
—Fandom Post

ROBYN HOOD: THE HUNT (2017)

LaToya Morgan (W) Daniel Mainé (A) Leonardo Paciarotti (C)

Robyn Locksley has finally taken down the monsters and villains that have plagued New York for far too long. Now, with the streets safe again, Robyn unfortunately isn't going to get to enjoy them. After being transported to an otherworldly, high tech, maximum security prison, she must fight for her life from some of the very creatures she has placed there.

ISBN: 978-1942275749

ROBYN HOOD: THE CURSE (2017)

Chuck Dixon (W) Julius Abrera (A) Robby Bevard (C)

After a daring and dangerous escape from a sadistic supermax prison, Robyn is finally back home where she belongs. But as she re-acclimates to her "normal" life in New York City, a new evil has been released and Marian Quin needs Robyn's help to send it back from where it came... But this battle is about to get more personal than either of these friends could have imagined, and nothing will ever be the same!

ISBN: 978-1942275817

To complete your Robyn Hood collection today, visit your local comic book retailer or www.zenescope.com